RAID AT RED MILL

by Mary McGahan

Illustrated by Ned Butterfield

SILVER MOON PRESS
NEW YORK

First Silver Moon Press Edition 2001
Copyright © 2001 by Mary McGahan
Illustrations copyright © 2001 by Ned Butterfield
Edited by Carmen McCain

The publisher would like to thank Dr. Judith Spikes of the
Larchmont Historical Society for historical fact checking.
Special thanks also to Larchmont Historical Society trustees, Joe Hopkins and
Eleanor Lucas; members of the New Rochelle/Larchmont Chapter of SCBWI
Writers' Group; and the librarians of the Larchmont Public Library,
whose unfailing help and interest made this book possible.

For information:
Silver Moon Press
New York, NY
(800) 874–3320

Library of Congress Cataloging-in-Publication Data

McGahan, Mary.
    Raid at Red Mill / by Mary McGahan ; illustrated by Ned Butterfield.-- 1st Silver Moon
Press ed.
        p. cm. -- (Adventures in America)
    Summary: Near the close of the Revolutionary War in 1782, fourteen-year-old Anne
Mott of Westchester County, New York, calls on her Quaker beliefs to protect her family
and property from British raiders when a long-time friend puts them at risk.
    ISBN 1-893110-11-7
    1. New York (State)--History--1775-1865--Juvenile fiction. [1. New York
(State)--History--1775-1865--Fiction. 2. United States--History--Revolution,
1775-1783--Fiction. 3. Quakers--Fiction. 4. Courage--Fiction.] I. Butterfield, Ned, ill. II.
Title. III. Series.

PZ7.M16715 Rai 2001
[Fic]--dc21

                                                                            00-047034

10 9 8 7 6 5 4 3 2 1
Printed in the USA

To my husband Frank
for all his support and faith
in this venture.

—MM

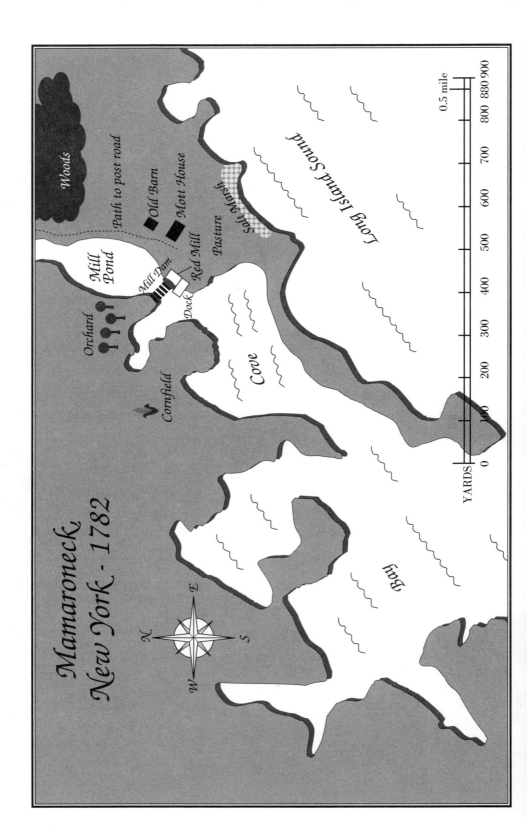

Mamaroneck
New York - 1782

Woods

Path to post road

Old Barn

Mott House

Mill Pond

Orchard

Mill Dam

Red Mill

Dock

Cornfield

Pasture

Salt Marsh

Cove

Long Island Sound

Bay

YARDS   0   100   200   300   400   500   600   700   800   880 900

0.5 mile

ONE

ANNE MOTT RACED HER HORSE HOME-
ward along the deserted post road. She could
see no trace of life in any direction. Grass grew
shoulder high in the surrounding fields, and tall
weeds filled the ruts from carriage wheels long
vanished.

Leaning precariously in the saddle, Anne
glanced back over her shoulder one last time to
make sure she wasn't being followed. Still seeing no
one, she cut off on the by-path to the family farm,
flew past the larch tree that marked its entrance,
and headed down the path to the mill.

Two horses stood outside the mill-door, saddled
and ready to go. Her brother Richard paced up and
down between them.

"I'm glad you're still here!" Anne gasped, out of
breath and barely able to speak. "I've just come
from the Quimbys'!"

As she reined in her horse, Richard came to her
side. He threw back his head and raised his eyes to
the sky. "What can you be thinking? Why did you
come by the post road?" he asked. "Hasn't Papa
warned you again and again to stay to the back roads
when you're alone?"

Anne looked down at her frowning older brother.

"I had reason! . . . I was in a hurry! . . . I wanted to see you before you left! . . ." She struggled to keep calm so Richard wouldn't think her childish but failed to keep the note of urgency from her voice when she continued with the disturbing news. "The Quimbys were raided last night," she said.

"Was anyone hurt? Was the house broken into?" Richard asked, concerned.

"No," Anne answered, "but the thieves took their last remaining cow and a whole cartload of corn."

"Well then," Richard interrupted, "I wouldn't call it a raid. It's only another petty theft like the ones we're bothered with all the time. So many folks are hungry . . ."

"Give me leave to finish!" Anne said. "The thieves weren't just local men! Josiah couldn't sleep last evening. A little past midnight, he heard a noise outside and looked out the window. He saw some figures creeping away in the darkness with his wagon. Then in a patch of moonlight, he recognized two of them!"

"And who were they?" asked Richard.

Anne waited for a moment to give her words full force.

"Fade Merritt's men!" she said, gripping the reins of her horse so tight they made a welt on the palm of her hand. She shivered as she thought of the notorious raider.

"I don't believe it," said Richard. "Everyone around here knows the Quimbys are Quakers like us. Even Fade Merritt knows better than to plunder people who take no sides in the war. Our old neighbor Josiah lets his imagination run wild."

"No, he does not!" Anne replied, dismounting from her horse at last. "Josiah's always been a sensible person."

"Fade would have to be desperate to come here," Richard responded. "I think you're making too much of this. The war has been going on for six years and nothing serious has happened to us."

"That's just the point," Anne said, leaning toward Richard with concern. "Fade may be getting desperate. Think of it. We've escaped the big raids so far. We've so much more left of everything than others in Westchester. So maybe he is after us now. And you and father are leaving!"

"Friend Josiah may be sensible for the most part as you say, but he's always been a bit of a pessimist too," said Richard with an air of finality.

Anne tossed her head. "Whether Josiah's a pessimist or not, I think he's right this time. He says this group was spying to see what provisions he had and grabbed what was easy to take. He's sure they'll be back with more men to raid his house and take every bit of food and clothing they have and every last stick of furniture. To say nothing of what harm they might do to the family!"

Richard's voice softened. "Be calm, Anne. You won't be alone here. You have the mill and farmhands. If there's any real danger, they can take a message to Cap'n Pete."

"But Cap'n Pete isn't always around. And if

Josiah is right, it'll be all the worse for us if Cap'n
Pete and his whaleboats are seen here from now on."
Her voice trailed away. She wouldn't give Richard
any further reason to think her cowardly. At fifteen
he was just one year older than she, but he often
acted as though he were the head of the family.

Richard shrugged his shoulders. "Papa and I will
be back before you know it. After all, Purchase is
only twelve miles away, and we're only staying a few
days. I must see what's keeping him," he said and
walked off into the mill.

Anne was troubled. Richard and Papa had their
minds set on this trip. It was to be the start of
Richard's ministry, and Papa was so proud and
happy about it. James Mott was a well-known figure
in the Society of Friends. He used his pen, his
money, and his influence to help put an end to war
and slavery, and he traveled widely to meetings to
speak and work for these causes.

If Richard didn't see the need to get Papa to call
off this trip, she wasn't going to ask him herself. And
if Richard were right that she was overly upset, it
would be wrong to keep him and Papa from a meeting that was so important to both of them.

Frustrated, Anne dropped Patience's reins and
walked to the stone wall nearby. The wall edged
the waters of the small cove on which the family
farm lay. It was quiet now. Only a gentle murmur
rose from the meeting of the waters with the rocks
below. Beyond the cove entrance, the larger waters
of Long Island Sound lay still and glass-like under

the blazing summer sun.

Not even the slightest breeze stirred the air. Anne wiped the perspiration from her face and began unpinning the long gray overskirt she wore to protect her dress when riding. The overskirt was all dusty now, but she folded it carefully and draped it over the wall in front of her. Removing her cap, she tossed her head about until her long brown hair fell loose and free.

The wall was Anne's favorite place to think and dream. She seated herself there now and gazed longingly across the waters stretching out before her. New York City lay to the south, well beyond the farthest point she could see. For the hundredth time her mind drifted back to memories of life as it had been there before the war—the warm brick house on Beekman Street always filled with company, her Quaker school just blocks away, her friends, Mama's smiling face.

Then suddenly when Anne was eight, Papa hurriedly sold the house and moved the family north to Westchester to escape the British invasion. Not long after, they buried Mama in the Quaker graveyard a few miles away.

Six years now it had been, six long years of learning to live without Mama's warmth and courage. Six long years of learning to live without her in this perilous place with no government or law, a place filled with packs of looting soldiers and roving bandits like Fade Merritt.

Papa had not foreseen that the British would drive

the American army right past them into northern Westchester, then withdraw their own forces back to the city, leaving the Motts in a "no-man's land" between the two armies.

"Here's Papa," Richard called, interrupting her thoughts. She turned to see him emerge from the mill. Papa was tall and handsome, with a look of authority about him. As he walked towards the waiting horses, he set a broad-brimmed white hat on his head and brushed off the mill flour that had settled on his plain gray outfit.

James Mott smiled at Anne as she approached and raised his eyebrows at her two younger brothers, who came rushing out the door behind him. He looked down at his two young sons and, firmly but kindly, put his hands on their tousled red heads.

"Robert and Samuel," James Mott said, "you are to obey your elders while I am away, your sister Anne especially. As I've told you before, Anne is in charge of the household now, and you must respect her wishes."

Robert, who at eleven was quite serious for his age, nodded solemnly. Samuel, the younger by two years and barely able to stand still for a moment, spoke up, "When can we go with you?"

"In a few years," said Papa, smiling again.

Anne hugged her father and then Richard. "Say nothing of the theft to Papa," she whispered into her brother's ear.

As they mounted their horses, Anne looked up at the two men of the family. How alike they were.

Richard was now as tall as Papa and blessed with the same handsome but serious face. She could see that their thoughts were already on the journey and the work ahead. They said their good-byes quickly.

"Don't stay over long in Purchase," Anne called after them, trying to make her voice firm and cheerful.

When they had moved out of sight and the boys had gone back to their chores, Anne picked up Patience's reins and led her back to the barn. The horse was a sorrel Narragansett pacer with a white star on her forehead. Papa had given her to Anne for her eleventh birthday, and they had traveled hundreds of miles together in the three years since. But now that she had turned fourteen, Papa had said it was time she stay home and learn how to take care of the household.

After unsaddling Patience and refilling her water pail, Anne took her overskirt and cap from the hook where she had hung them, and walked up the path to the house. Richard was right about one thing. She had been a fool to risk the post road this morning with such a beautiful horse.

Papa had warned her to use only the back roads when she was alone, and in her hurry she had not heeded him. People often called her headstrong, and they were right. But if Josiah was correct about Fade Merritt, Patience would not be safe even here in her own barn.

Anne found it impossible to sleep that night. The August heat made her room stifling. She paced the floor, peering out the window into the darkness outside, her ears alert for any suspicious sound.

For hours images of the dreaded Fade Merritt flooded her mind. She'd heard he was a giant of a man with shaggy black hair and fierce coal-black eyes, his left arm cut off at the elbow. He had lost the arm in a fight.

As the night wore on, the images grew more vivid. Any small doubt Anne had earlier in the day about the presence of the villainous bandit in the area vanished. Even though little harm had come to the family thus far in the war, she was certain that Richard was mistaken about Fade Merritt.

First thing tomorrow she'd send for Adam Mott, who lived across the water at Cowneck on Long Island. Adam was kin to her, and they had always been particularly good friends. She knew he would take her concerns about Fade Merritt seriously and maybe give her some advice. She scribbled a quick note to him, wondering if he would sense what she did—the increasing danger around them.

Two

ANNE ROSE EARLY, TIRED FROM HER uneasy, sleepless night but too anxious to stay in bed longer. From her bedroom window on the second floor, she could see beyond the cove and the Sound waters to the low green hills of Long Island on the opposite shore.

The aroma of coffee wafted up from the kitchen. Hurrying downstairs, she found Grandmother Underhill, spectacles on her nose, squinting over her work at the spinning wheel.

"Sit down and have something to eat in peace before the boys come down," Grandmother said. "I left a stack of griddle cakes warming."

Anne reached into the brick oven at the side of the huge fireplace, flipped a few of the cakes onto her plate, and seated herself at the long kitchen table. The air in the room was stale and hot. The white curtains at the windows hung limp and motionless.

Anne was just spreading a thin layer of apple butter on top of a griddle cake when Grandmother announced, "Cap'n Pete's coming tonight, and he's bringing his daughter with him."

Captain Pete was coming tonight? Tonight of all nights, with Papa and Richard away, and Fade Merritt's men on the prowl? Anne couldn't think of a worse time! She jumped up from the table, clutching the note she had written last night.

"I'll be right back, Grandmother. I must tell Jess something," Anne called over her shoulder as she hurried from the kitchen and out to the mill. Jess ran the mill for her father. She was sure he would find a way to get her message to Adam.

The earth was dry from lack of rain. Tiny puffs of dust rose from Anne's feet as she ran. The open door of the old red mill was as inviting as always. But its water wheel was motionless now and the huge millstone silent.

So many of the surrounding homesteads were abandoned these days that customers were few. Anne missed the constant bustle of farmers arriving full of humor and gossip, their carts piled high with wheat and corn.

Inside the mill, Jess was taking advantage of the lull. He had the huge millstones apart and was picking the grooves to keep them rough for grinding whatever grain came in the days ahead. The tedious job had been going on since yesterday.

Anne wove her way through piles of sacks and barrels to his side. "I've had some upsetting news," said Anne. "The night before last, it seems some of Fade Merritt's men stole the Quimbys' cow and a cartload of corn. Have you heard any word of him from our customers?"

Jess stood, put aside his tools, and stretched his dark arms above his head. "Folks are always gossiping about Fade Merritt," he said, "but I've heard nothing lately."

"I think we need to get in touch with Adam. I've written him a note. He may be able to help us."

Jess nodded. "Best to see what he thinks about the situation. I can spare one of the millhands to sail across to Cowneck, but it will be slow-going with the wind down. It's bound to take more than an hour each way."

Returning to the house, Anne pushed aside the griddle cakes. They were cold now. She was in no mood at this moment for eating anyway—or for spinning two pounds of flax, either, but that was her share to do each day.

"I'll take over the spinning, Grandmother," she said, reluctantly.

The older woman settled into her rocking chair with knitting she had taken from a box by the hearth. Anne sat in front of the spinning wheel, but her mind was elsewhere. Despite all intentions to keep her worries from her grandmother, she found herself blurting out, "I think it's time Papa stopped Cap'n Pete from sailing his whaleboats from here to trade in the city! He's crossing British lines without permission! That's treason, and it's treason for us to support him!"

Grandmother, surprised at Anne's outburst, hesitated before responding, "I'm sure your father continues to allow Cap'n Pete to sail from here because he feels it's worth the risk to help people around here get what they desperately need. Remember how he saved the Hamill baby's life last year with medicine he got in the city?"

Anne nodded. Trading food for manufactured goods had been lifesaving for them. But it was more than that with Papa. She knew that, deep in his heart, he, like herself, favored the American cause. She'd heard him grumble about the injustice of the king's taxes and laws. But away from his own house, he kept quiet for the family's safety.

Her fingers felt stiff and awkward as she began to spin. She worked for a while in silence, then abruptly stopped. It was too hard to concentrate on anything else right now, when more than ever she was aware of the danger of the family's position. Just a few miles south, the British outposts defended New York City by land, and the dreaded British guardship stationed at Throgs Neck defended it by sea.

"We're so close to the British lines with all their Tory spies and sympathizers, word will pass to Fade Merritt in an instant if the whaleboats are seen leaving here tonight. If the British don't catch Cap'n Pete first, Fade Merritt will, and he'll have every reason to raid us for helping him!" Anne said.

"Don't fret so, Anne," Grandmother replied, "your father doesn't involve himself in Cap'n Pete's activities beyond letting a valued former worker sail his boats from here once in a while. No harm should come to us from that."

"Cap'n Pete does more than sail his boats from here," Anne said. "He expects a hearty welcome when he arrives and food and lodging when he returns. And he hides his whaleboats in the millpond when he wants. The whaleboats are hidden there right now!"

At this third outburst, Grandmother put her knitting aside and rose to put her arm around Anne's shoulder. "Be calm," she said.

It was not proper for Anne to continue arguing with her. Frustrated, she began spinning again and changed the subject.

"Did you say Cap'n Pete was bringing his daughter with him tonight? I've not seen Rachel since the day Cap'n Pete came looking for work at the mill right after we moved here. I'm surprised. Why do you think she's coming?"

"She's planning to make the trip to the city," Grandmother replied, taking up her knitting again.

"You mean Rachel's going along with the men in the whaleboats?"

"Yes, Rachel is going—and her mother too. They're used to hard work, to life on the water as well as on land. Of course, Cap'n Pete didn't want them to go along with him. It's a dangerous trip, I grant you, but Rachel was determined to find some fine cloth for her wedding dress."

"Rachel's getting married?" Anne asked, surprised.

"She's sixteen now. It's high time she started her own family." Grandmother hesitated for a moment, and then said thoughtfully, "You're fourteen, Anne. You'll make someone a good wife in a few years."

"How did you find out about Rachel?" asked Anne. "I haven't heard of a wedding in a long time. Life's been so lonely here since most of our friends moved away, and the Sunday Meetings were canceled."

"Cap'n Pete sent a message to Jess at the mill late last night, and Jess brought the word to me early this morning," said Grandmother, putting her knitting down in her lap again and looking intently at Anne. "I guess you'd rather be traveling with your father than sitting here spinning."

"I would. I love going to new places and meeting new people," she said, remembering wistfully all the journeys she had taken with her father before he had put her in charge of the household. "There's so much need—so many people still in slavery, so many widows and orphans because of the war. And I'll miss riding Patience on the long journeys to New York and Philadelphia."

Grandmother nodded. "I understand that, but you were lucky to have had all those opportunities to travel safely in such dangerous times. Not many fathers are so well respected that they have passes to go through both armies' lines."

"Well, I prefer traveling to staying home," Anne interrupted.

"But now it's time you settled down, dear, and learned to run a household like Rachel." Grandmother shook her head, "You look so much like your mother did at your age—so tall, with the same blue eyes and dark hair—sometimes I think I am talking to her again. She was also restless like you, but once she married your father she was glad she had learned household skills. You are now a young woman and must learn to sit patiently and spin a fine thread as well as you ride a horse," said

Grandmother with a twinkle in her eye. "Later on, you can go back to the Friends' ministry. Many of our women do. You know that."

"I'm sure Mama would have," said Anne quietly. Despite Grandmother's last words about sitting patiently, she rose and went to the window. She wanted to get a breath of air even for just one minute, some relief from the stifling heat inside, and a glimpse of a wider world than the four walls of the room and its boring spinning wheel.

In the filmy haze of morning, farmhands were harvesting salt hay down by the meadows that rimmed the east arm of the cove. Some were cutting the hay, some were turning it to dry in the sun, and some were loading big fork-loads of the dried crop into carts to be pulled to the farmyard. There, it would be neatly stacked in an open shed with a thatched roof to keep it dry. *Good fodder for Patience*, Anne thought.

"What time is Cap'n Pete coming?" she asked, returning to the spinning wheel.

"Near sundown, as always," Grandmother answered.

The whaleboat trips had been going on for years. From what Grandmother said, Papa would need good reason to stop them. Had she known Captain Pete was coming tonight, she would not have hesitated to tell Papa about the theft at the Quimby farm. Now she would have to wait until his return. Even though she was in charge of the household, the mill and Captain Pete were, after all, still his business.

THREE

AS THE DAY PROGRESSED, ANNE WAS filled with growing concern. Jess's millhand had brought word that Adam would not be coming until tomorrow, and any hope she had to speak to him before the whaleboat expedition that night was lost.

To make matters worse, she learned Jess was going along on the trip to the city. He was a strong patriot and loved to sail with the whaleboatmen. "I'm going to hunt up some ducks to sell in the city tomorrow," he called as he walked by the front door towards the marshes near the Sound. "The millstones are all in working order, and there's not a customer in sight."

After he returned in the early afternoon with close to a dozen ducks, he went fishing for the evening's meal. As Anne watched him head off to the fishing boat, she thought of how much he was like his father—lean and strong and kind. How she had missed Jess's parents after they retired to a small house a few miles away!

The elderly couple had been slaves in Anne's mother's family until just before the war when New York members of the Society of Friends agreed that Quakers must free their slaves. By then the old couple had been with Anne's mother's family so long, it seemed the better, or even the only, choice they had was to stay with them. They moved in with Anne's mother when the Motts settled in the country.

For as long as Anne could remember, they were like kin to her. And through long evenings by the fire, she'd heard the tragic stories of slavery. She'd heard the happier tales, too, of life in Africa before they had been captured and sold.

Anne was glad that Papa had never held slaves himself, and at home he had given testimony to his beliefs by banning any slave products, such as cotton or coffee, from being used there. Coffee made from peas was a poor substitute, but it was worth the sacrifice.

Upset as Anne had been when Jess's parents left, her heart lifted when Jess took over the mill and brought home to the farm a lively young wife named Jinny, just a few years older than she. They moved into a small house attached to the mill.

Today Jinny was busy all day away from the house, and Grandmother was feeling somewhat poorly. The hours passed slowly, and Anne found it hard to concentrate on her chores. She was shelling peas from the garden when she heard the slow trot of one of their old farm horses as it pulled the family cart down the back lane to the farm. *Must be Jinny come home from berrying at the Wilsons'*, Anne thought.

In minutes the young woman was at the door. Slim and tall, with a bright red kerchief around her neck to offset her plain homespun dress, Jinny walked briskly into the kitchen. Like her mother-in-law she always wore a Quaker cap in tribute to the family's stand on slavery. She plunked down two huge baskets of blackberries on the table.

"Jess will have plenty of food to sell in the city tomorrow," she said. "We can sort these berries into smaller baskets later. Now I'd best get right away to cooking this mess of fish Jess caught."

As she began boning the fish, Jinny turned to Anne, her eyes shining. "The Wilsons have asked me to make Rachel's wedding dress."

"I'm not a bit surprised," said Anne delighted. "Everyone knows you're the best seamstress around." The girls chatted on until the smell of bluefish frying brought the family to the table. They were complimenting Jinny and Jess when they heard the sound of voices outside the house.

Robert and Samuel jumped up from the table. "Cap'n Pete is here! Cap'n Pete is here!"

"Feels like a storm may be brewing!" Captain Peter Davis boomed out as he came in the door. He was a big broad-shouldered man, bronzed from the sun and his days on the water.

"Evening, Mistress Underhill, Mistress Anne," he said, in his rapid-fire way, sweeping off his weather-beaten tri-corner hat and bowing courteously to Anne's grandmother and then Anne. "Evening all. Two little fellows behaving?" he asked, nodding to Robert and Samuel.

Rachel slipped through the door behind her father and stood quietly while he made his greetings.

How she had changed! Her childhood plumpness was gone and her bright red hair had softened to auburn. And beside her stood a sturdy young man, his blonde hair bleached almost white by the sun.

"I'd like you to meet my daughter Rachel and her husband-to-be," said Captain Pete, gesturing to the couple, his broad face beaming.

"But Anne and I have met before," Rachel said quickly. "It was six years ago, though—I counted just this morning. Remember, Father, I came with you right after the Motts moved here? It was the day you came looking for work at the mill."

Anne nodded. She remembered it well. They'd had a lot of fun that hot summer day.

"Jess, whaleboats ready?" Captain Pete broke in.

"I've been doing some repairs on one of 'em, but it's fine now."

"Need to look at 'em. Got the extra men for me?"

"Yes, I got three. All's ready," replied Jess eagerly.

"We'll have our full ten men for each boat, then," Captain Pete remarked with satisfaction.

"Men?" asked Rachel. "How about Mother and me?"

"Sorry, daughter. Just a manner of speaking," Captain Pete assured her. "What are you taking with you to trade this time?" he continued, addressing Jess.

"I've got ducks. And I'll have Jinny's berries. I sure can use the money. For one thing, I'm almost out of shot for hunting . . ."

"All right then," interrupted Captain Pete.

"Tide'll be favorable around midnight. Looks like the weather's on our side, and there'll be no moon tonight. Men should be here after eleven. Come along, John," he added to Rachel's beau. "We need your help now."

With that, the three men moved out of the house toward the mill. Robert and Samuel tagged along behind them. Jinny remained in the kitchen sorting the berries into smaller baskets.

"Cap'n Pete," Anne called, following him and quickening her pace to keep up with the seaman's long strides. "There's been a theft at the Quimbys', and Josiah saw two of Fade Merritt's men! If they are around and learn you are here, I know there will be trouble."

"Seen in every nook and cranny of the county that bandit is! Every place at once! Can't live my life by rumors!" Captain Pete said, kicking a large stone in his path clear over the wall into the water.

"Please take precautions, Cap'n Pete. I'm worried . . ." Anne didn't know what else to say.

"I am always cautious, Mistress Anne," he said amiably and moved on.

Anne looked after him, frustrated, but turned politely to Rachel, who had followed her from the house. "Why don't we sit here a while," she said, pointing to her favorite spot on the wall near the water.

"I heard what you said to my father. I think you worry too much, Anne," said Rachel, sitting down. "There's always talk of Fade. People think he's everywhere."

"If Josiah Quimby is right about Fade Merritt's men, the talk must be taken seriously now," Anne said.

The August sun was close to setting, and it was almost fully obscured by low-gathering clouds. Anne was glad for the coming twilight. She looked back over her shoulder, uncomfortable that Captain Pete and his men might be seen working on the boats just upstream from where she and Rachel sat.

"You should not go tonight," Anne said, placing her hand on Rachel's arm. "Why risk such a trip now? You could end up on a British prison-ship in New York Harbor, and that would be the end of your wedding and probably your life. Aren't you the least bit concerned?"

"I'm a little nervous. Still, I want so much to have a good dress for my wedding—even if it means buying British goods—and even though the trip is dangerous. The few dresses I have are worn and patched like this one." Rachel moved both hands down over the rough brown homespun cloth of her outfit.

Anne could see Rachel was too preoccupied with the dress and the wedding to see anything at all clearly. She shook her head at the girl's stubbornness.

Quaker clothes were simple and plain. Most of Anne's dresses were somber gray, made from linen Grandmother and Jinny had woven themselves. Anne had learned not to want anything fancy, and she wondered if a dress was worth risking your life.

FOUR

THE TIME FOR THE WHALEBOATS' DEPARture came soon enough. Close to midnight the entire sky was cloudy, and a night breeze was stirring. Captain Pete preferred, when possible, to sail on a moonless or even stormy night so he would not be seen. Tonight the dimmed lanterns of the crew gave the only light in the inky darkness.

Anne and Jinny walked to the dock with the boxes of berries. Rachel's mother had just arrived with the last of the men. She'd brought baskets of eggs and butter. Rachel stood by her side. Anne's brothers sat on the edge of the dock, their legs dangling over the side. No one spoke.

Anne could barely see the men as they pulled the boats from their hiding places in the marshes along the millpond. The pond had been formed by damming the small stream that flowed beside their house. A sluice by the side of the dam could release the water into the cove to turn the big mill wheel. Other sluices under the dam made it possible to release the pond water when it was too high.

The pond's marshes made a safe private place for the whaleboats to be hidden. The men worked in silence. The slightest sound, even the distant call of a whippoorwill, made them pause to listen and peer into the darkness around them. In minutes they hoisted the boats to their shoulders and moved stealthily along the marshes and around the mill until they were below the milldam. Then they lowered the boats into the deep waters of the cove and tied them to the mill dock.

Anne counted eighteen men present, along with Rachel and her mother. With only the dim light of the lanterns, they carefully wrapped their precious baskets of food in oilskin and placed them under the seats of the whaleboats. The boats were about twenty-five feet long and about five feet broad in the center, so there was ample room for storage.

Anne had heard Captain Pete brag about how well these boats were put together. Made of light wood, they were easy to maneuver and carry if necessary. He said they were called whaleboats because they looked like boats used in the whaling industry: "double-enders," boats with both ends pointed.

At last ready to go, the men snuffed out the flames inside the lanterns. Captain Pete stood by the steering oar at the stern of one boat, and Rachel's fiancé stood at the stern of the other. The oars were muffled with cloth so they would not make groaning noises against the oarlocks. Swiftly now, with no sound at all, the boats moved off through the cove entrance into the black waters of the bay that opened into the Sound.

Anne watched until she could no longer see the outline of the boats against the gray sky. A screech owl startled her. For a moment she thought she saw

a light flicker beyond the orchard, but it was gone in a second. Despite the heat of the summer night, she felt a distinct chill.

"It's long past your bedtime," Anne told Robert and Samuel as they walked back toward the house. Jinny had gone off to her own little rooms attached to the mill.

"Oh no, not yet," they protested. Anne knew how excited they were.

"You can stay up and read a while," she said.

Inside the house, Anne took two lighted candles from the kitchen table, handed one to Robert, and led the way upstairs with the other. She saw her brothers to their room.

"Don't stay up too long," Anne said from the doorway.

Robert sat at his desk to consult his almanac for the next day's weather. Samuel tapped him on the shoulder, eager to continue talking. Wondering if they'd be able to sleep at all, she moved out into the dark hallway.

Her candle cast strange shadows on the walls. She looked in on Grandmother. She was fast asleep and faintly snoring. Anne blew out the candle before entering her own room. She wanted to be able to see outside.

As she took up her watch at the bedroom window, she wondered why Adam hadn't come today. It was so dark, Long Island might have been across the great ocean for all she could see.

The night breeze rustled the leaves on the trees

and bushes outside. She had been in her chair only a few minutes when she heard a soft knocking at the downstairs door. Heart pounding, she crept out to the head of the stairs.

"Anne, Anne," Jinny's voice came in a hoarse whisper.

She ran down the stairs and opened the door.

"I just heard men's voices. I think they're creeping away across the milldam," said Jinny. "They must have been hiding in the marshes when the whaleboats went out and been poking around here since."

Anne was filled with dismay, but she tried to act calm. She thought for a few moments before speaking. "Jinny, stay here in the house with Grandmother and the boys. Those men might come back. I'm going to take Patience to the shed in the woods."

"No, don't go off in the dark alone. You're more valuable than Patience," protested Jinny.

"I'll be careful. I know the path well. Don't worry," Anne said and left quickly before Jinny could protest again.

In minutes, Anne was in the barn and had placed a halter on Patience. Whispering softly to quiet the horse, she led her out to the hidden path that started between two chestnut trees.

Anne moved cautiously. Familiar as she was with the path in the daylight, it seemed different at night. The darkness gave her cover but made her passage difficult. To make matters worse, the path was overgrown and purposely left that way for secrecy.

Anne tried to ignore the briars and thorns that

tore at her legs and the dry scratchy leaves that brushed against her face. Distracted by a cobweb that caught in her hair, she tripped over a large tree root and fell, wrenching her ankle badly.

After about ten minutes, she finally saw the dark outline of the shed and with relief led Patience inside. The agitated horse gave a low snort and a toss of her head. Anne gently removed the bridle and whispered soft words into the animal's ear.

When Patience had settled down, Anne sank onto the floor and leaned back against the wall of the shed to rest a while. She took off her shoe and rubbed her ankle, hoping it wouldn't swell.

In the deep blackness of the moonless night, she could see barely more than a few feet. The loud drone of locusts and crickets made it impossible to listen for the sound of a snapping twig or a cracking branch. Frustrated and weary, Anne put her head down in her hands. Fragments of what she'd heard about Fade Merritt from customers at the mill began to nudge at her memory.

Fade Merritt had once been part of a ruthless band of raiders called the Refugees—men who spent their days and nights stealing cattle, horses, and everything else they could find for the British army—and just as often for themselves. The British found Fade so cruel they'd dismissed him. Now he roamed throughout Westchester on his own, robbing and pillaging "the Rebels," as the Americans were called.

Anne lifted her head and straightened her shoulders, determined to put away such thoughts. It didn't help one bit to terrify herself here in the middle of the forest, when she still had to make her way back to the house. After she was sure Patience was accustomed to the shed, she rose and limped her way home warily through the dark thickets.

"I'm back," she said to Jinny.

"All's been quiet here," Jinny answered. Reading Anne's concerns, she added, "I'll get Patience at first light."

"She'll need some care. She's probably scraped up worse than I am," said Anne.

Jinny nodded. "I'll sleep upstairs in Jess's mother's old room. I'll feel safer there with Jess gone—and don't worry—I'll tend to Patience first thing in the morning."

The two young women looked at one another and turned together to bolt the door. Anne was glad for the company.

She slipped quietly up to her room and lay wearily on her bed. Her ankle throbbed and her scrapes burned. But she was in no mood to attend to them now.

The waters in the cove washed rhythmically against the stone wall below. The ancient sound usually soothed her to sleep, but tonight it gave her no comfort. Someone had been out there watching.

FIVE

ANNE GOT UP AT DAWN. SHE WAS STIFF and her ankle still throbbed, but she was relieved that the night had passed without further event. From her window she could see that the water in the little cove looked gray and a bit choppy. The gentle breeze of last evening was growing stronger.

Anne hoped the breeze meant the beginning of release from the heat and that Adam would be able to sail across Long Island Sound more quickly this morning. She could take the boys for a sail and meet him at the cove entrance.

Carefully she washed her hands and face with water from the bowl that stood on the chest close to her bed and attended to the bumps and bruises from the night before. Then she changed into clean clothes, adding her freshly starched best white cap and apron, and went down to the kitchen.

Robert and Samuel were already eating breakfast, too excited to sleep late. Grandmother and Jinny were stirring large bowls of cornbread batter for the meal that would celebrate the safe return of the whaleboatmen. *If there is to be a safe return*, Anne thought.

"Did you get Patience?" Anne asked Jinny.

The older girl nodded. "She's safely back in her stable. I saw no trace of strangers around."

"I wonder what the Wilsons and Jess are doing now?" Robert asked.

"Their wares are probably sold already and the money jingling in their pockets," said Jinny.

"And they have a long day ahead to spend it," added Grandmother.

Anne looked at her brothers. "How about a sail this morning?"

"Yes! We finished a new corn crib yesterday," said Robert. "I can go out for a while."

"Jess said I won't be needed at the mill this morning," said Samuel with great importance.

"I'll be back to help you with the spinning as soon as I can," Anne said to her grandmother as she bundled up a few peaches in a napkin.

The small family skiff was tied up by the mill-dock. Robert and Samuel ran ahead and raised the sail. Anne gathered up her gray skirts and hopped lightly aboard.

"Let's go over to the Sound side," said Robert, pointing to the eastern arm of the cove on which the farm lay. It was a long curving spit of land covered with pine trees and wild shrubs, which protected the cove from the rougher waters of the Sound. It could just as easily be reached by walking from the house. But the boys loved the boat.

The sail billowed out in the stiff breeze. Moving out from the mill dock, the three reached their destination in a matter of minutes. The boys jumped into the shallow water and soon disappeared into the thickets bordering the shore, heading for the beach

and the Sound on the other side. Anne saw that they were carrying sacks for their shell collections.

At other times these brief outings with the boys had been opportunities for quiet thought, provided Anne remained in the boat as she did today. She lowered the sail and sat quietly, lulled by the gentle rocking motion of the water.

From her position, she could see a good part of the farm. It was a view she had grown to love. North of the cove, her two-story white home crowned the top of a low hill. To the west of the house stood the old red mill, and across the milldam lay the fruit orchards and the cornfields. To the east stretched the green pasture where their now lone cow grazed peacefully.

"Look. There goes a British ship," Robert's voice carried to her on the breeze. "Let's get it."

"Into the whaleboat, men," cried Samuel.

Anne snapped to attention. The boat had drifted away from the shore without her realizing it. What had happened to the shell collecting? Why were the boys suddenly playing marauding whaleboatmen? What had they been hearing at the mill?

Anne's thoughts suddenly turned somber. The British controlled Long Island. She had seen Tory sloops, filled with livestock, grain, and firewood from the island farms and forests, moving along the southern part of the Sound close to the Long Island shore. Day after day she saw these supplies move down to the British army and the people in the city.

And from time to time she heard that Americans

in whaleboats from Westchester and Connecticut, on the side of the Sound where the Motts lived, attacked the sloops and carried off their cargoes. It was an act of high treason to the British. What if the British confused Captain Pete and his harmless trading missions with these whaleboat raiders?

"Anne, Anne," Robert called, interrupting her thoughts. "Adam's coming!"

Anne stood up quickly, raised the sail again and steered toward the cove entrance, the narrow opening where the two curving arms of the cove came together. The boys had run there to jump into the imagined whaleboat. Now they were waving wildly to Adam. He was their favorite relative. He sailed with them, fished with them, and told them tall stories.

"Get into the boat, and we'll sail in with him," Anne called to her brothers. They scrambled down a tall pile of rocks, hauled themselves aboard, and together they waited for Adam's arrival.

Minutes later Adam drew up beside them.

"We'll race you to the dock," called Robert.

Adam laughed. He had the advantage of already being in motion and was at the dock first. In seconds he tied up his boat with expert hands and reached down to help Anne ashore. She looked up at him as he climbed from the boat. How tall and dashing he looked even in his simple homespun clothes.

Turning to Robert and Samuel, who were eagerly awaiting his company, he said, "Sorry. No games today. I've only a short time, and I must spend it with your sister."

Disappointed, the boys accepted his answer grudgingly. "When are you coming back?"

"I don't know," Adam answered. "But next visit I'll make sure I have more time. I promise."

"You had no problems coming across?" asked Anne, looking up at him. Growing as tall as she had lately, she still barely came to his shoulder.

"No, I was fine. I'm always careful when I have to cross by day, but I wasn't going to wait 'til another nightfall to get to you. Jess certainly didn't wait 'til dark to get your message across. The Tories have better things to do than bother small unarmed sailboats, but it's not wise to take chances unless you have to."

SIX

ADAM AND ANNE WALKED ACROSS THE milldam, which separated the millpond from the cove, and turned into the apple orchard. The sound of heavy grinding stones in the mill had just stopped, and only the lazy drip of water from the slowing mill wheel could be heard.

They seated themselves under the shade of one of the largest trees and leaned back against its trunk. "I'm sorry I couldn't come yesterday," Adam said. "Shadow had just developed a case of colic when Jess's messenger arrived."

"Jess didn't tell me that!"

"I didn't want to upset you. I know how fond you are of horses."

"I'm sorry, Adam," Anne said. "You shouldn't have left him." She abandoned the small hope she'd harbored that Adam could stay until the whaleboats returned. She would not dream of allowing him to leave his priceless horse at such a time.

"He's in good hands. I called in Ben Watson. He knows more about horses than anyone on Long Island. I'm worried about Shadow, Anne, but I came because I'm more worried about you," Adam said softly. "Ever since I heard your brother was going off to work with your father, I thought you'd be alone here too much."

Anne looked up quickly. So he had worried about her before she sent the message. This was something different, something personal. She noted as if for the first time how his thick chestnut hair fell over his forehead and how kindly he looked at her with his dark brown eyes.

"Yes, it's suddenly become a worry," she said. She hesitated a moment, reluctant to add to his concerns back home and hardly knowing where to begin.

Adam broke into her thoughts, "Tell me about this business with Fade Merritt," he urged, leaning forward.

Anne started out slowly but, encouraged that he was taking her seriously, recounted all of the events of the last two days and poured out her fears.

When she had finished, Adam shook his head. "I don't wonder that you're so concerned," he said. "I'm upset about the way things are going myself." He stood up and paced back and forth. "When the British surrendered at Yorktown last fall, I thought things would be better here. Yet almost a year's gone by, and we're still persecuted by these raiders. Refugees, Skinners, Cowboys, whatever they're called, and whether they're on the British side or the American, they're a vicious lot of scoundrels."

"I wish my father would be as aware as you," Anne said.

"Just remember," Adam reassured her, "having James Mott for a father is no small thing."

"I know he's an important man, and his neutrality has kept us safe so far. Everyone knows he keeps no arms here on the farm except for hunting. But he's away so often I don't think he knows what's going on around us right now. He thinks conditions are improving."

"Conditions are improving everywhere but here." Adam replied, sitting back down and folding his arms. "New York is the last place the British will give up, but even they know the war is coming to an end. Old Josiah may well be right. Fade Merritt and others like him will be greedier than ever to get what they can before their day is finished."

"If that day ever comes," Anne said.

"Meantime," said Adam, standing again and looking all about the farm, "I think some precautions must be taken here. I don't see as many of the mill or farm hands around as usual. Where are they?"

"Cap'n Pete was short of men, so three of them went along with him."

"This won't do at all," said Adam, angrily. "It makes the situation here doubly bad. It's a small farm, and you don't have that many workers to begin with. I think now perhaps I should stay, Anne."

"Absolutely not!" she shot back, standing to face him but wishing she could accept his offer. "The whaleboats will be back a few hours after midnight, and I'll be all right until then. I'm more worried about the days ahead if these expeditions keep up!"

Adam considered her reassurances. "I hate to

leave, but I'll send three of my best workers over as soon as I get home. I'm sure they'll be a comfort to you toward nightfall. I'll be back as soon as I can, probably the day after next, and I'll try to talk some sense to Cap'n Pete and your father. It'll be hard for your father to keep his old friend from what he may think is necessary business. But Cap'n Pete shouldn't take even one of your workers. That's not safe for anyone."

Anne was somewhat relieved that there would be a few more men about, but she couldn't help worrying still. She nervously smoothed out her apron. "I'm responsible for my family, and I want to keep my head when danger comes."

Adam placed his hand on Anne's arm. "You've always impressed me as brave. Even daring. When you were only eleven, you managed to hide a herd of cows from raiders. You didn't run when you heard they were nearby. Your first thought was to drive the cows into the woods behind the house."

"That's because I wanted to hide Patience, too. I was young then, but I think I was braver then than I am now."

"It's more complicated now than when we were children, isn't it?" Adam said. "I don't think I used to be as aware of danger. But now we're old enough to know what can happen if we're not prepared for it." He hesitated as if he suppressed something he wanted to say. They were silent for a while.

"I don't want to keep you any longer," Anne said reluctantly.

"My mother sent something for you," Adam said

smiling. He took a spotless white linen handkerchief from his pocket. From it he unfolded two beautiful silver combs.

"Your mother left these in our house years ago before the war. My mother came across them only last week. She remembered they were important because your mother wore them the night she promised to be your father's wife. Mother wanted very much for you to have them back," Adam said, his fingers closing over Anne's as he placed the combs in her hands.

Again, they stood still and silent for a few moments, looking into each other's eyes as if some pact had now been made between them. Then suddenly the whole mill structure shuddered as the mill wheel groaned to a start, and whooshing water to a steady beat brought the silence to an end.

Wordlessly, they walked back to the dock. Anne watched until Adam sailed out of the cove's entrance.

She ran to the spit of land where the boys had played earlier. The Sound was grayer and choppier now. She watched until Adam's boat disappeared in the mist that hung over Long Island.

At a quiet protected spot among the rocks, she sat down to think. So Adam Mott really cared specially for her, not just as the little girl he had played with from childhood. He was eighteen now and ready to start thinking about marriage. Adam and she were related on her father's side, but the relation was distant enough that she knew it would not be a problem if they wanted to get married.

In her mind, she went over every bit of the conversation with him again and again. She was almost sure now that if he was thinking about marriage, he was thinking about marriage with her. Slowly she fell into a happy reverie.

Meanwhile, the light breeze of morning turned stronger, sending cool air eddying around her. Seagulls swooped over her head, moving from the Sound to the safety of the cove. It was a signal for bad weather ahead. As Anne started for home, her eye caught something out on the water.

Just above the low mist-covered hills of a small nearby island called Whortleberry, she saw the tall masts of a big sailing ship slowing to a stop. *It can only be a British ship*, she thought.

It was the closest any such ship had ever come to shore here. This was indeed something to be feared—something Captain Pete couldn't know to expect on his return. *Worse for him . . . and for us,* Anne thought.

Seven

THAT EVENING AFTER ROBERT, SAMUEL, and Grandmother went to bed, Anne and Jinny made final preparations for the whaleboatmen's return. They were expected a few hours before dawn.

Anne and Jinny would have to make do with the little food they had on hand. Together they set the long kitchen table for twenty guests. They piled pewter plates high with Jinny's cornbread, covering them with linen cloths to keep the food fresh. There'd be fresh peas and some fried pork. There'd be no tea because it was taxed so heavily by the British—only the coffee made from peas and sweetened with maple molasses. A little butter, perhaps, for Jinny's cornbread. And of course, cider . . . and for a treat, peaches.

The meal preparations were long finished when Jinny dozed off in the rocking chair by the fireside. Anne tiptoed upstairs and found both boys asleep in their clothes. She let them be.

Back in her room, Anne was grateful for the presence of Adam's men, who had come before nightfall as promised. Throwing herself down on the bed for the few hours before the whaleboats' return, she closed her eyes to rest them. Despite all good intentions, she fell sound asleep.

Sometime just before daylight, she awoke. Bursts of rain hit the windows, and a strong wind howled around the corners of the house and rattled the shutters. Immediately she realized that something was wrong. The boats had not returned.

Downstairs, Jinny was sitting in the chair by the fireplace, rocking rapidly to and fro.

"Did you stay in the chair all night?" Anne asked.

"No, I went up to rest in bed for a few minutes but couldn't sleep. I just kept pacing the floor and praying and praying all night."

"Are they almost here, do you think?" Anne asked.

"I hope so," Jinny whispered, rising and going to the window though nothing could yet be seen. "They'll be caught if they don't come soon. They'll end up on a British prison ship. Or some villain will sell Jess into slavery. What use will our freedom be then?" Her hand shook as she stirred up the fire's dying embers, and tears poured down her cheeks.

The room was silent now except for the sound of rain and wind.

Jinny drew herself up and wiped her cheeks. "I'll start to cook the meal anyway," she said. "There are too many bad things in this world for me to be crying over something I don't even know has happened."

She and Anne had worked in silence for the better part of an hour when their thoughts were interrupted by the boom of a distant cannon echoing and reechoing across the water. It was a familiar sound, but an ominous one. Something had drawn the attention of the British guard ship at Throgs Neck.

In seconds, Robert and Samuel came down the stairs two at a time. "We heard a cannon," they shouted.

Jinny and the boys bolted outside. Anne grabbed a few cloaks off the hooks at the hall-door and followed. Grandmother, awakened too, stayed behind and calmly took over the cooking.

They ran as fast as they could down the long, curving east arm of the cove to the cove entrance where Anne and the boys had met Adam the day before. Adam's men and the remaining workers came running behind.

The ground was muddy from the heavy rain, and they slipped and slid in the gray light of early morning. Out of breath and covered with mud, they scrambled to the point where the land ended in a high bluff of rocks that guarded the cove entry. On the west a large bay indented the Westchester shore; on the east the waters of the bay met the rougher unprotected waters of Long Island Sound.

"I can't see anything," said Robert.

"Neither can I," said Samuel.

The wind was fierce, and the rain slashed at their faces. Though it was summer, they shivered. Time passed slowly, and the full light of early dawn was upon them when Robert cried out, "I can see them! I can see them!"

Samuel's mouth flew open. For once he was speechless.

Anne looked across the bay to where her brother pointed. There Rachel's mother stood at the steering oar in the lead boat, and behind her in the second boat stood Rachel.

The boats hugged the shore. As they pulled behind the last island before the land curved inward with the bay, the rowers seemed to pause for a moment as though Captain Pete thought for them to stop there. Then suddenly from behind the marsh grasses along the shore next to the boats, a group of men ran to the water's edge and began firing on them.

"Raiders!" Anne cried as she watched the boats pull out away from the safety of the land. Plain for all to see, they had no choice but to cross the mouth of the bay and row directly towards the cove entrance.

The northeast wind was now blowing a gale. The boats pitched and tossed in the rough water. Waves broke over the bows, showering the rowers and threatening to swamp the boats at any moment.

"Oh, look, look," Jinny yelled.

Anne froze. Robert was pointing to the British ship she had seen the day before. Anne felt a lump in her throat as she watched it now come into full view from behind Whortleberry Island. To her dismay, she saw it was a fighting brig—a square-rigged, two-masted warship turning rapidly towards them in full sail. At its stern the ominous British flag whipped in the wind.

No wonder Captain Pete had hesitated to come out from the shore and cross the bay. He must have seen the brig before they did. It was only a matter of minutes to safety behind the long east arm of the cove, but the British ship had already moved into firing range of the whaleboats.

"Look at the men on the bow!" cried Samuel. "They're going to shoot the long gun!" Immediately, one cannonball after another began to rain down around the whaleboats. But the rough waters affected the British, too. The brig rolled enough to spoil the gunners' aim.

"Get down!" Anne yelled, pulling Robert and Samuel from the top of the rocks into safety below.

"We can't see the brig! We can't see the brig from here!" they protested.

"Better not to see than to be killed," she cried. "Just keep your eyes on the whaleboats. That's good enough."

Anne could see the boats well now. Everyone's clothes were soaking wet. Their bodies strained to pull the oars faster and faster. Captain Pete shouted orders that could barely be heard over the roar of the guns.

"Hurry, hurry, come on, come on," Robert and Samuel yelled.

Jinny stood silent, her face masked in fear.

The brig fired faster and closer. One cannonball hit the large rock at the land's end just as the boats darted behind it and into the cove. It fragmented into splinters that rained down on the rowers, but they were safe now. They rested their oars and let the boats grind to a stop on the gravelly shore. Exhausted, they sat at their stations, heads in their hands, unable to move.

Anne grabbed the cloaks from beneath the sheltering rock where she had flung them and handed one each to Rachel and her mother. The two sat in their separate boats exhausted and shivering, unable to catch their breath or speak. Jess had already stepped quickly from the boat with his packages and was walking arm in arm with Jinny back along the long arm of the cove towards the house.

Anne slipped away. As rain and wind slashed at her, she climbed back up the slippery treacherous rocks to the very top of the bluff, hoping to see that the brig hadn't sent out a smaller boat in pursuit of the whaleboatmen. For a few moments, as the brig moved towards shore, Anne feared the worst. To her relief she saw it was only making a wide turn to pull away from the shallow, reef-strewn water near the cove and move back behind Whortleberry Island. On the shore side the gunmen had disappeared.

"They've gone!" Anne cried. She scrambled back down to the rocky shore and bounded into the boat with Rachel and her fiancé. Robert had taken over a vacant oar abandoned by one of the most tired of the crew. To his consternation, Samuel was struggling to share the oar with him.

Rachel was motionless. "You must be exhausted," Anne said, forgetting her own tiredness. "Let's get back to the house." Then taking her place at another vacant oar, she helped row across the cove to the mill-dock to unload. Assisting the weary rowers was an old custom at Red Mill.

EIGHT

"WHAT HAPPENED, CAP'N PETE?" Robert asked when they were all seated around the long kitchen table, the precious parcels stashed underneath the benches.

"Tell us, tell us!" demanded Samuel.

"Give Cap'n Pete time to catch his breath," said Anne. She filled mug after mug with cool cider for the thirsty travelers, while Jinny served large platters of food from the steaming pots in the fireplace.

But Captain Pete was eager to begin his tale. Everyone else gulped down the food, too hungry to talk.

"You see two of our company missing. Don't need to name them. Almost brought disaster," Captain Pete growled. He pounded his mug on the table with each word, splashing cider in every direction.

Robert and Samuel were so awed by Captain Pete's fierceness that for once, neither interrupted.

"All went well in the city. The wife sold the eggs and butter at a tidy profit. With the money she bought the new iron pot she's needed so long. I got some rope and caulking for the boats. Jess got his gunpowder for hunting. And Rachel found her cloth," he added, obviously pleased. He stopped for a bite of pork and continued.

"Dusk came, and we headed early for the marshes and the trip home. Three men missing! We waited for hours. Our nerves and temper grew worse by the minute. Then one of the blokes showed up tipsy from drink."

Anne rose to refill everyone's mugs.

"No time to wait," Captain Pete continued, quickly downing the cider. "Tide and wind were against us. We pushed out of the marshes into the water. Headed for home. Left the rascals to fend for themselves!"

"Hear, Hear!" roared the whaleboatmen, pausing to respond between bites of food.

"We reached Throgs Neck and our crossing place. It was almost daylight. We jumped from the whaleboats and carried them to the other side faster than ever. Watch on the British brig saw us and called out. Drums rolled—first time in our travels to the city," he said, again pounding his mug on the table.

"We heard the guns," said Robert.

"That's what woke us up," added Samuel.

"The brig hoisted full sail right away," Rachel interrupted. "It was only a short time before it rounded the point of Throgs Neck and began firing its cannon at us. We needed every man to row, so Mother and I took the steering oars. In minutes we were behind the islands along the way and fairly flying in the shallow water near the shore where the big brig dared not follow."

"Fine job you both did," Captain Pete responded. "Proud of you both. Responded to all my directions. Missed every rock and shoal."

He pushed aside his plate with a clatter and took over the thread of the story. "As we neared the cove, we rowed slowly. Thought we were safe. Behind the last small island, thought to rest a while. Enjoy our escape. And what's waiting there?"

Captain Pete was talking faster than ever, leaving out even more words than usual. When he paused for breath, Anne answered his question. "Raiders were waiting there. We're in danger here now for sure!" she exclaimed.

"No, Mistress Anne, no trouble here. They want us, not you. After we leave, you're safe. They'll follow us. Don't worry."

"Hear, hear," yelled the whaleboatmen, now also hitting the table with their mugs. Finally, Captain Pete called for an end to the eating and drinking, rose, and beckoned the men out to the barn for a nap.

Towards evening, Rachel and her mother came downstairs from Anne's bedroom where they had been resting. Rachel brought with her the precious package for which she had almost lost her life. Anne had forgotten all about it.

Jinny, Grandmother, and Anne gathered around as Rachel opened the oilskin-covered package and drew out lace, embroidery thread for the trim, and yards of pale blue silk.

"Beautiful," Jinny murmured, fingering the fine fabric. "I can't wait to get started."

Anne smiled. Even though she was still content with her own simple fashions, she was happy that Rachel would soon have so lovely an outfit for her wedding.

"The stores were almost empty," Rachel said excitedly. "We searched everywhere. But finally we went to Hanover Square and found this." She held the silk up proudly. "It cost a fortune, but it was worth it."

"Beautiful," Anne and Jinny murmured.

"We must be going now," broke in Rachel's mother. She was a woman of few words, eager now to get home to her usual routines. "I cannot thank you enough for your hospitality to my husband all these years."

After the whaleboatmen had moved the boats from the dock back up around the mill into the marshes surrounding the pond, the Davis family left quickly on horseback. With them went Captain Pete's comrades.

Even though the workers who had gone with Captain Pete were back, Anne was glad that Adam's men were still there as well. Her fears were now more grounded than ever. At last, some Tory group had seen the whaleboats returning here. Those men firing from the shore this morning—were they Fade Merritt's men? Captain Pete said they'd be interested only in him. He was wrong. Danger was closing in on the Mott farm. She felt it in her bones.

NINE

DESPITE ANNE'S FEARS, THE WEEKS THAT followed were quiet and ordinary. The work of the mill and farm went on. The memory of the theft at the Quimbys' and the attempted attack on the whaleboatmen began to fade like vanishing ripples in the millpond. Even Anne grew a little complacent.

Papa and Richard returned and left again. The men who had fired on the whaleboatmen from the nearby shore were identified as a few local Tory sympathizers emboldened for the moment by the presence of British warships, not Fade Merritt's men. Papa didn't consider the episode serious enough to keep Captain Pete from his work.

And Adam managed the visit he'd promised. Thanks to his advice, none of the Mott workers went off with the whaleboatmen again. Adam's own workers had returned home and his horse had recovered. Captain Pete came less often and usually didn't bother the family when he did, except when he brought Rachel to be fitted for her dress. Jinny had fashioned the blue silk into an elegant gown and was now embroidering tiny pink roses onto the lace that would trim the neck and sleeves.

Meanwhile, summer was moving toward autumn. The sun slipped farther south every day. Soon the trees and shrubs that rimmed the cove would be turning red and gold.

Anne and Grandmother sat in the parlor one hot September morning, idle for a few minutes after breakfast. A rare letter from one of Grandmother's old friends in the city had somehow gotten through the lines by post-rider only that morning.

"What does Mistress Bailey say?" Anne asked.

"Food and other goods are in very short supply in the city. She says attacks on British shipping interfere with getting any supplies from Long Island," Grandmother said. She put down the letter and looked at Anne. "I'm glad we're here in the country. At least we have our own milk and eggs and vegetables and fruits, not to mention fresh fish."

"Given that piece of news, we're more in danger of a raid than ever," said Anne, her complacency gone in an instant. "Every whaleboatman will be a suspect in the attacks, including Cap'n Pete. And even if Richard and Papa were here, we've no way to defend ourselves."

Grandmother folded up the letter and gave Anne a studied look. Calm and composed as always, she spoke softly, "If danger comes, our defense will be our courage and our witness to what we believe. You can't control life. All you can do is what is right. And what is right for us is not to bear arms. Some must sacrifice and show a different way to peace."

Anne nodded solemnly in agreement. She rose to look out the window. Robert and Samuel, at leisure for the moment, were perfecting cartwheels on the lawn. A broad patch of cove water shimmered in the sun, and the smell of fresh-mown hay drifted up from the salt marshes along the cove.

How can I protect those I love? she wondered. Something about the situation at the farm bothered her, but she couldn't explain it in words.

Restless, she excused herself and left the house for the mill. The boys saw her and followed.

"Cap'n Pete's here. We wanted to talk to him," said Robert.

"But Jess said he's sleeping in the barn," interrupted Samuel.

Anne saw the two whaleboats tied at the dock. She headed for the mill and Jess.

Jess met her at the door. "I'm worried," he whispered.

"Why?"

"Cap'n Pete and his men captured a Tory sloop off Long Island last night, and I didn't even hear them come and go!"

"They captured a Tory sloop?" Anne was shocked. Captain Pete was doing more than trading!

"Yes! A sloop loaded with hay, a few sheep, and food supplies for the city. They took the sheep and supplies, and burned the sloop!" Jess shook his head. "He's got the sheep and the food in the barn. Worst of all, he let his three prisoners off in New Rochelle!"

"They let the crew off in New Rochelle?" Anne was stunned. "So near here?" How could they be so careless? Word would spread like wildfire!

She hurried out the mill-door to look around.

Jess followed. "Oh, no! Mistress Anne, look over there," he said.

About twenty men were scrambling down from horses in the cornfield.

"Fade Merritt and his men!" he whispered.

"How do you know?" Anne whispered in return.

"From what I've heard, I'd know him anywhere. Run for the house."

"Robert, Samuel, come quickly."

"Why, what's happening?"

"We're being raided!"

They raced down the path toward the house. Once inside, Anne slammed and locked the door. Her heart was pounding. She cried a warning to Jinny and Grandmother in the kitchen. Then she ran toward the boys who were already at the parlor window that looked out at the mill and the barn.

Several whaleboatmen, rubbing their eyes, came stumbling out the barn door into daylight. Their clothes were askew and their hair uncombed. They hobbled along trying to put their boots on as they moved.

It was too late.

Some of Merritt's men moved across the milldam and onto the dock. Two of the bigger ones kept a tight hold on Jess. Others jumped into the whaleboats to check their contents. Anne's heart, still pounding, now skipped a beat as she saw what they were finding and holding aloft with cries of triumph. Muskets! Canisters! No doubt filled with powder and shot! How dare Captain Pete bring arms to a

Quaker farm!

Jinny joined Anne at the window.

"Jess is done for. He's done for," she gasped. "Cap'n Pete is caught by surprise."

"No! Look!" Robert said, pointing to the garden. Behind a picket fence lined with currant bushes, all of the whaleboatmen, fully awake now, stealthily approached the mill from the barn, and they had guns! They fired a volley of shots up into the air and kicked up the dry dust of the road so the enemy could not detect their numbers.

Dropping their spoils, Merritt's men jumped from the whaleboats to the dock and back onto the mill-dam. They ran across it to the other side of the cove, where their leader and the rest of his band were waiting. The two holding Jess released him and ran as well. Jess ran to join Captain Pete's men.

The whaleboatmen moved quickly. Some continued to fire. Others jumped into the whaleboats and pushed them through the sluices under the milldam and up into the millpond behind the dam. Grabbing the ammunition from the boats, they scrambled onto the shore and headed into the mill. With lightning speed, they opened all the windows facing the mill-dam and trained their guns on the enemy.

Fade Merritt sat astride his horse watching it all, caught by surprise, like the rest of his men. Anne shuddered. He was worthy of her worst nightmares. A huge, fierce-looking man, he rested his gun on what remained of his left arm, ready to fire. Instead he dropped from his horse, furious at his men for

retreating and leaving their guns on the bridge.

"Follow me," he roared and flung out a string of curses as he moved towards the milldam.

At that moment, Captain Pete's voice boomed out over the water. "Fade Merritt, stop right where you are, or I'll take you before the hangman can!"

Fade kept coming.

"I won't stop at your bidding, Peter Davis, you thieving Rebel," he said, flinging out another string of curses. "I've found you out at last. Robbing British sloops, eh? I might have known."

"If you won't stop at my bidding, then you'll stop for my gun, you cursed Tory! Another step will be your last," bellowed Captain Pete.

"Come out, you sneaking thieves. Come out from where you're hiding," screamed Fade, not daring to advance any further.

"Fade, you infernal cutthroat, if you don't leave now, I'll save you from the gallows by shooting you."

"I'll not move an inch for you, you Rebel swine."

"Fade, if you don't go off this instant, this gun will go off."

Anne's fingers gripped the windowsill.

"He's turning around," yelled Robert.

"He's leaving," yelled Samuel, jumping up and down.

"He had no choice," said Anne.

"Thank God," said Grandmother and Jinny together.

They watched as Fade Merritt climbed up on his big roan horse, and his men followed suit. Bellowing back more curses, they rode away from the cornfield.

As quickly and as irresistibly as the water from the millpond poured out when the sluice gate was opened, the truth of her situation now rushed in upon Anne. Up to this moment, she'd let herself be lulled by everyone else's false sense of security.

She had been right to be concerned. The others were wrong—Richard, Grandmother, Captain Pete. Not Adam. He had not tried to talk her out of worrying. But he could not be with her every moment.

As soon as Fade and his band had moved out of sight, Anne strode out to the mill, where the whaleboatmen were praising Captain Pete for his stand.

Anne stood tall.

"Captain Peter Davis," she addressed him in solemn tones. "You put us in grave danger here. You know we're Friends and reputed to be a peaceful family. It was dangerous enough that you crossed British lines to trade illegally in the city. But now you have committed an act of war."

"Mistress Anne," he said proudly. "I kill no one and keep no prisoners. All I do is deprive the British of goods that keep them here longer than we want. A peaceful act of war."

"The British won't consider it so. As I just said, you put my family at great risk. Already you've drawn greedy-eyed men here to see what we have. Now Fade Merritt has every excuse to punish us for letting you sail your boats from here. I can't allow you to do this any longer. In my father's absence, I am responsible for this decision."

"I'll respect your wishes in the future," Captain Pete said in his politest tones.

"Very well then," said Anne, "but we are in danger now, and I want you to stay until my father returns."

"No need to worry, Mistress Anne. Fade Merritt is after me. It's plain to see. I humiliated him today. He's enraged. He wants his revenge on me, and soon. If I stay, he'll be back with more men to get me and maybe attack the house as well. If I leave, he'll follow me tonight, and you'll be let alone. It's the only way you'll be safe!"

Captain Pete's jaw was set in a stubborn line, and Anne knew from experience there was no convincing him otherwise. He headed back for the dock.

Anne sank down at her favorite place on the stone wall near the mill. The boats were set to leave around midnight. She felt sick to her stomach. There was no way out for her. She must face great danger alone. The farmhands and millhands would be there, but she would be the one responsible for dealing unarmed with whatever situation arose.

Fade Merritt would come back to this farm so untouched by the war. He would come here before he went after Captain Pete. Anne wished now that she had stopped Captain Pete that first night after the robbery at Quimbys'.

What a fool I've been, just waiting around and worrying, she thought. She would take whatever measures, however limited, she could in good conscience take. Now.

TEN

ANNE SLIPPED AWAY TO THE HOUSE. THE parlor was empty. Grandmother must have gone up for a nap.

The sunbeams were slanting through the parlor window and falling on the tall mahogany clock that had chimed all the hours of her childhood. She walked over to it, opened the glass door in front of the clock face and traced over the numerals with her fingers.

So many minutes, so many hours, had passed since Mama died. Anne stood in a reverie for a long time. When she snapped shut the small door, it was as if she had closed the door of her childhood forever.

Turning, she decided to assess what she could save.

Upstairs, the large wooden chest in the hall was filled with all the family's sheets and blankets. Smaller chests in the bedrooms held their clothing. The linen bedding and clothes were made from flax grown right here on the farm. Anne's stomach tightened as she thought of all the weary work it had taken to make them—the planting, harvesting, refining, spinning, bleaching, weaving, dyeing, cutting, sewing.

And there was more. Anne went to her room and

sat on the bed to think. In a matter of minutes all the things the family had taken months and months, even years, to create and collect could be taken away or set afire and destroyed.

"I have something for you, Anne," Grandmother called from her room.

Grandmother sat in a large comfortable easy chair by the window, holding the big family Bible on her lap. As Anne approached, she opened it to the front pages. Squinting a bit, she traced down the lines of her family's forebears until she came to the name of her daughter Mary Underhill and the record of her marriage to James Mott in 1765.

"This Bible would have been your mother's," she said, looking up. "I was saving it for your wedding, but you must take it now."

Anne looked back at her grandmother. "Thank you," she said, kissing the older woman on her forehead. She walked slowly back to her room with the heavy book in her arms.

Anne opened the Bible carefully and found Mama's name again and the date of her marriage. How she wished she could have talked to Mama about that day, but she had been too young to think about such things before Mama died. For a while she tried to imagine how her own name would look linked with Adam's on the next line of the page. Then she lay the book gently on the table next to her bed.

As soon as Grandmother and the boys had retired for the evening, Anne enlisted Jess and Jinny in her plan to foil Fade Merritt. She couldn't save everything in the house, or even very much. It would be physically impossible for them to do so and too obvious even if they were able. But she could save small and precious things like the Bible.

Using no candles in case they might be watched, she led Jess and Jinny down the long hall at the back of the house to a small workroom at the end. Moonlight cast strange shadows as Jess pushed her mother's beautiful wedding chest along the floor. The front of the chest had been painted with the Motts' wedding year, their initials, and bright red tulips on either side.

"Be careful," Jinny cautioned Jess. Quickly they moved aside the old loom in the corner of the workroom and the small carpet on which it stood. Underneath was a hideaway—a space reached through a trapdoor and completely separated from the cellar. When they opened the door, a musty smell escaped. The family had never used the space, and Robert and Samuel had not been told of its existence.

"Hurry," said Anne, anxiously. With great effort the three of them lowered the heavy chest through the opening and down the rickety steps, straining not to drop it.

Anne went up to her parents' bedroom for the smaller items she had in mind to hide. First, she would take her mother's most loved possessions: her inlaid sewing box; the expensive fan Papa had once brought her from Philadelphia; her favorite basket with the crewel work she had been doing while she was sick; the beautiful carved cherry till-box, empty now, that she had once given Papa as a present. Anne's hands shook as she folded them all into her large apron.

There were so many other valuables she wanted to hide that she could not move fast enough. In the heat her hair grew damp against her cheek, and the palms of her hands sweaty as she carried the best of the tableware to the hiding place—the blue and white china and the silver. She added a few sheets and blankets, two small tea tables, and several of their best mahogany chairs. Nothing very large.

Last of all she placed in the wedding chest the silver combs that Adam had given her. Later, she would put in the Bible.

Back in her room, she felt a headache coming on. She peered out her window but could see nothing in the darkness. She lay down on her bed and tried to compose herself but could not.

She was surprised to hear Grandmother enter the room. "I don't sleep very well anymore, so I must tell you I've heard something strange going on in this house. What is it?"

"Grandmother, don't worry, I'm just taking a few precautions. I've hidden some of our most precious things. Is there anything you want to hide?"

"The Bible, to be sure. Not that raiders would be interested."

Anne had always wondered if Grandmother had only tried to console her by putting down her fears about a raid, and now she was sure she had. Grandmother had always known they were in danger.

She had wanted Anne to at least see the Bible before it was too late.

"It might get damaged, so yes, I'm going to hide it," Anne replied.

"Down in the hideaway?"

"Yes."

"That's all I care about," Grandmother said and left the room without another word.

Anne lit the candle on the table next to her bed and picked up the Bible. There would be no sleep for her this night. Her fingers shook a little as she searched the pages for her favorite heroines. They had been examples of strength for her since Mama died, and she read and reread their stories until dawn.

As the first light appeared in the East, Anne snuffed out her candle and crept downstairs with the Bible. Slipping quietly into the hideaway, she placed it in the chest with the silver combs, came back up, and pushed the loom back over the trapdoor.

All night she had prepared herself in mind and heart for the coming confrontation. She remembered her Grandmother's words. "We will keep no arms— ever, and if danger comes, our defense will be our courage and our witness to what we believe."

She had thought of hiding Robert and Samuel downstairs as well, but if the hideaway and all the valuables should be found, the raiders would be so angry they might harm the boys. She had made other arrangements, and she would make the boys part of them now in a way that they would not suspect the worst.

ELEVEN

"ROBERT, SAMUEL," SHE WHISPERED. "Wake up!"

They turned over, drowsily. "What's wrong?" Samuel muttered.

"We have a serious task to take care of right now, and I need your help. I'm worried that some of Merritt's men might have seen Patience here yesterday and will come back and steal her today."

"What can we do?" Robert asked, sleep leaving his eyes as he jumped up quickly from his bed. Samuel rolled over and looked at her with startled eyes.

"You know that small shed hidden way back in the woods?"

"Yes, we play there a lot."

"Jess has already gone there with some hay, a bucketful of oats, and pails of water for Patience. He's going to put some straw bedding down as well."

"You're going to hide Patience there?"

"No, you are!"

"We are? When, when?" they asked, their voices filled with excitement.

"Right now. Jess must be back at the mill by now. I'll tell him it's time for you to go," Anne answered. "You mustn't return until I come for you. Is that understood?"

"Yes," they replied, filled with importance.

When Anne came back from the mill with Jess, she hugged the boys and watched them from the back door. In the dim predawn they moved out into the woods, leading Patience by the reins. Robert was carrying his almanac and diary, and Samuel his silhouette of Mama. *They know!* she realized. Anne shivered despite the heat.

Grandmother, in the kitchen earlier than usual, had not slept either. Jinny had come over with Jess. She and Grandmother were as resigned as Anne that a raid was coming but determined to go on with the day's work as though nothing were happening. They had already begun making bread.

"It could be days," Jinny said, her hands covered with flour, "or it could be any moment."

As daylight gradually crept through the windows, Anne heard the millstones grinding and the wheel turning. Jess would not stop his labors either, despite the threat that hung over them. She paced the parlor floor, eyes fixed on the parlor window.

By noon the mill wheel no longer moved. Off in the cornfield some of the farmhands harvested corn, working slowly in the heat. The birds were quiet. A lone cricket chirped a sad note in a bush outside. Three swans barely moved across the glassy cove. The whole outside world seemed to have stopped.

It was early afternoon when she saw them—a band of armed men, maybe a dozen or fewer this time—creeping through the apple orchard toward the mill. Her knees went weak as she watched the huge figure of Fade Merritt lurch forward through the mill-door with the others following quickly behind.

"They've come." Her voice broke as she called to Grandmother and Jinny in the kitchen. "They're in the mill. The house will be next."

It was not long before noisy footsteps grated outside, and a heavy hand pounded on the door. Anne opened it to a hulking man with a musket slung over his shoulder.

"Fade Merritt wants to ask you some questions. He's in the mill."

Seizing Anne's shoulder, the hoodlum shoved her out the door and toward the mill. The dreaded moment was at hand. Anne, strengthened anew in her Quaker convictions and fiercely determined to show no cowardice in the face of violence, went along quietly.

When her eyes became accustomed to the darkness inside the mill, it was all she could do to control the panic that sparked within her at the sight of the ruffians around her. For the first time she saw the villainous Fade up close. He towered over her, his black eyes cold and piercing, his handless arm dangling at his side. Behind him, his men stood staring at her, guns at their sides, their faces hard.

The floor to the right of her was stained with blood. Jess's blood? What had they done with him? Where was he? She choked down a sob.

Anne's eyes moved back to Fade. Next to his shoulder hung the noose of a rope, which was slung over a ceiling beam. He began to speak to her in a quiet but menacing tone.

"We know there's money somewhere on this farm with all the goings on here. I just heard a big shipment of corn was stored here a short time ago. You won't be harmed, young miss, just so's you tell me how much money you got for it and where that money is."

"I don't know," Anne replied.

"You must have heard your father speak of it."

"I heard about the shipment but not the money. American officers confiscated the corn, and if they paid for it at all, it probably was with useless paper. That's all I know. I've had little to do with my father's business up to now."

Fade jabbed a bony finger into her shoulder. "Come now Miss, be that so, James Mott is a rich man. He must have other money here. You must know something about it."

"I know nothing."

Fade's patience was short. He pushed his face close to Anne's, dark eyes bulging as he spat out his words. "Money!" he said. "You know where it is, and you'd better tell me."

"I don't know, so I cannot tell," Anne repeated.

"Then we'll find a way to make you tell the truth," he threatened.

"I have already told you the truth."

Fade motioned one of the men to put the noose around her neck. Anne flinched in terror, but from somewhere deep inside of her, she summoned the courage to keep her voice calm and even, "You must not touch me!" she said.

The man stopped for a moment, surprised, and let the noose drop.

"If you don't tell, we'll stretch your neck!" Fade thundered.

"If I can't tell you anything while I'm alive, I surely cannot after you hang me," Anne replied in a loud clear voice.

There was silence.

Anne knew Fade could easily kill her, but, her courage growing, she looked him in the eye. "You know I speak the truth. I know nothing about any money."

The men stepped aside to talk. Anne heard the whispers. "This one can't be frightened."

"It's no use."

"We shan't get anything out of her."

Fade, now in a rage, strode out the mill-door toward the house. "We'll find that money," he shouted back over his shoulder, "and if we don't, we'll find other things to make up for it. You Motts deserve to be punished for your treasonous ways with Captain Peter Davis!"

His men brought around the horses they had hidden behind the barn and drew the family cart up in front of the house. In the cart was Jess, blood on his face and clothes, a prisoner but alive! He had been forced onto the driver's seat and told he would take all the family goods away. He held his head and shoulders high though he did not know what fate would befall him.

Behind Jess they piled all their loot as they ransacked the house looking for the money: dumping drawers, breaking open chests with their gunstocks, ripping apart mattresses and pillows with their bayonets, flinging all the books in Papa's library from the shelves and trampling them.

When they didn't find any money, the raiders were furious. They took every bit of undamaged bedding, every piece of clothing, whatever furniture the cart would hold, and many small valuables that Anne had not hidden away.

And as they worked, they ate all the food they could, and took the rest—the last of the pork in the barrel, a sack of flour, the last pig, and the few remaining chickens. One man carried out the bread that had been baking in the oven and another a wheel of cheese.

Up to this point Anne had stood by watching in frustration. But at the sight of the man running off with the cheese, practically the only food soft enough for her grandmother to eat, she could no longer contain herself. She ran up and snatched the cheese from the man's hands.

"You will not take this. It's for my grandmother, and I won't let it go," she said.

Laughing derisively, he let her keep it.

Her anger rising, Anne turned now to Fade Merritt. "You know my father is a Friend and does not believe it is right to fight, yet you take the opportunity of his absence to do what has been done,

when only women are in the house!"

"Tell Cap'n Pete I said 'Hello,'" roared Fade, ignoring Anne's outburst as he mounted his horse. "And if I find him here again, I'll burn this house to the ground and the mill with it!" Riding to the front of his men, he ordered them to move out.

"It's over," Anne said quietly but stood trembling as she realized the terrible danger she had just escaped. The men had gone to the cellar looking for signs of fresh digging in case the family had buried valuables there. But they had not found the entrance upstairs to the hideaway.

Grandmother was pale. Jinny, her favorite chair gone, slumped down on the floor by the kitchen fireplace, silent, but with tears rolling down her cheeks. No one could console her.

TWELVE

THE NEXT DAY WAS HEAVY WITH CONCERN for Jess's welfare. The mill-hands went in the morning to search the countryside for word of his whereabouts but learned nothing. With sad hearts, Grandmother and Anne set about putting the household back to order but convinced Jinny to rest.

That evening, the family sat in the living room, fearful that Fade Merritt might return. The fears had increased with the gathering darkness, when in the distance, they heard the sound of horses approaching.

Robert ran to the window. "It's Papa and Richard," he cried.

"And Jess is riding double behind Richard!" yelled Samuel with delight.

Jinny was first out the door and was immediately caught up off her feet by Jess in a huge hug. As soon as he put her down, she swept him back to their rooms for the few scraps of food she had salvaged from the garden.

Anne looked up at Papa on his horse. He had slumped back in the saddle. His face was pale and his eyes wet. "We just found Jess walking along the road. He told us what happened," said Papa, his voice husky. "I feared what we would find here, but I see you are all safe." A smile began to curl the corners of his mouth, and he breathed a huge sigh of relief.

Richard was obviously upset. He swung down from his horse to give Anne a hug. "I'll always be ashamed that I took your worries so lightly. I'll never do that again," he said.

"Not for a while, anyway," she laughed.

"What an outrage that you had to endure such a terrible ordeal," said Papa when they had entered the house. He put his arm around Anne's shoulder. "Jess told me how brave you were. He heard what you said to Fade. They tied him upstairs in the mill, and your voice carried well." Papa smiled again.

"I never thought I would have the courage that came to me at that moment. I was so afraid."

"Being afraid doesn't mean you're a coward. It's how you act that counts. You gave witness to our Friends' beliefs yesterday. Without arms, you faced down an enemy who could easily have killed you. I'm very proud of you. I know someday you will serve the ministry well."

"I hope to, Papa," Anne said, smiling happily.

"As for Cap'n Pete," continued James Mott, "he's grown careless and must use another spot for his base. It's my fault. I wasn't paying enough attention to what he was doing. You were already in danger from the whaleboat trading, and whaleboat warfare took it one step further.

"I thought it was safer here because the war was winding down," he continued, "I should have realized conditions might get worse here in Westchester with the raiders that have plagued us all these years. I doubt Fade Merritt would have harmed a Mott, but then you never know what such a brigand might do."

"Papa, before Fade Merritt's raid, I reminded Cap'n Pete of our position as Friends. I asked him not to use the millpond anymore. I took it upon myself to do this."

"You did well," he said. He shook his head as he ran his finger down the long scratch on the side of the tall clock. "They didn't need to damage what they couldn't take," he said.

"I wonder what's left of my room," said Richard. He ran headlong upstairs.

Robert and Samuel were no longer able to hold back their part in the big adventure.

"Papa, we saved Patience!" said Robert.

"We hid her in the shed!" said Samuel proudly.

"Good work," said Papa. "Surely they would have taken such a beautiful animal."

"You can be proud of your children," Grandmother said. "They are strong people. The boys saved Patience, and I don't know what we'd have done without Anne. She protected her two brothers from a miserable experience, and she saved a lot of valuables as well. She put them downstairs in the hideaway."

"What hideaway?" asked Robert.

"Come along!" Papa said, taking a candle.

The boys were amazed that they had never found such an exciting place themselves. How could they have missed that opening under the rug, under the old loom? They plunged down the old stairway following Papa.

Anne followed down the steps and picked her way to the dark shadowy corner where she had placed her parents' wedding chest. Triumphantly she took the candle from Papa and held it high as she opened the lid to reveal the chest's contents. The boys gasped with surprise.

Papa looked inside curiously, then suddenly spied the tillbox in its hiding place next to the Bible. A broad smile crossed his face.

"You can explore all this later," he said to Robert and Samuel, "but now I want to show you something. Let's go back up." He held the tillbox under his right arm as he climbed the shaky stairs.

Anne wondered why her father was so happy all of a sudden. When they returned to the living room, the three children and Grandmother surrounded Papa, who had seated himself on a badly damaged sofa.

"You outsmarted old Fade," he said, drawing a wad of linen from the till. He loosened the small roll of fabric to unfold a handful of gold coins.

"I didn't see that," said Anne surprised.

"It has a false bottom," he chuckled. "I packed the money tightly in as much linen as would fit so that it would not make a sound when it was moved. It's money I saved from before the war. It gives me great satisfaction that you outwitted Fade, even though," he continued, placing the box on a table, "it won't ever make up for the terror they caused or

the destruction they wreaked here. And as for the corn shipment, Fade was wrong. I never received any payment for it, only promises."

Papa arose, square and tall and serious. "Now, justice must be done. I'll not let Fade Merritt get away with this," he continued. "I've heard General Guy Carleton is in charge of one of the British outposts here—Valentine Hill. His role is eventually to oversee the British departure from the country. It's said he's a reasonable gentleman, and if he'd been in charge, there'd have been no war. I'm certain he will hear my case and see that our goods are restored."

"The British are leaving?" Anne asked, her heart lifting.

"Most won't admit it yet, but I think it will be sometime in the months ahead," said Papa.

"I'm going with you to see this man," Anne said. "That's something I would like to tell my children about."

"We'll set out first thing in the morning," Papa answered. "But for now, is there anything to eat in this house?"

"Some cheese," Grandmother winked at Anne.

Outside, the rain poured down, and a cool breeze came through the parlor windows. Anne went down to the hideaway and retrieved the combs and the Bible. She placed them on the table near the window in her room. Picking up the combs, she tried them in her hair. She wondered what Adam was doing in his house across the Sound.

THIRTEEN

"THE KING'S SON IS WITH GENERAL Carleton at Valentine Hill," Papa told Anne. They were riding south together on the post road and then west toward the British outpost. It was a glorious sunny morning; the air was cool, and Patience, groomed to perfection, bent readily to Anne's gentle handling.

"What is the name of the king's son?" asked Anne.

"William Henry. He's King George's third son. Soon to be leaving with Admiral Digby's fleet. Maybe today you'll see a future king."

"But he won't be our king!" said Anne.

"I think not," said Papa.

They had been riding for over an hour when they reached the pickets guarding the Valentine Hill outpost of the British lines. Papa's papers gave them easy access, and they were directed toward General Carleton's headquarters.

Anne was astounded at the size of the encampment. As far as her eye could see, there were rows and rows of tents and soldiers marching in neat columns.

"There are thousands of them," said Papa. "It must be because of the prince."

A tall sentry led them into the white clapboard farmhouse, seated them in a small anteroom, and took Papa's message in to General Carleton. It was almost twenty minutes before the general came to the door and greeted them. He was splendid in his scarlet coat and gold epaulets.

"Mr. Mott, Mistress Mott, come in. I am sorry to have kept you waiting, but the prince's presence here keeps me busy. I have little time. Please tell me your business." General Carleton took a chair at a desk opposite them and folded his hands.

"Our home was raided in my absence two days ago by Fade Merritt, one of your ex-Refugee raiders," Papa began solemnly. "My daughter's life was threatened and my house ransacked. We have little left but the clothing on our backs. I have come to ask your help in restoring my possessions."

"I am sorry for your trouble," the general replied. "We can control our soldiers for the most part, but it is another matter to hold in these roving thieves that make a pretense of being our allies. I'm sure you know they have no loyalty to anyone but themselves. However, I will send soldiers back with you to locate this Merritt and warn him to desist from bothering you further. They will also have instructions to locate and restore your belongings."

"No soldiers," Papa answered firmly.

"No iron men for a Quaker, eh?" asked the general.

"Just give me a letter ordering my goods to be restored."

"Easily done." The general gestured to an aide to

go off and write the letter.

"Mistress Mott, I apologize for the ugly treatment you have received in our name. It is most distressing."

"Thank you," Anne replied. "But tell me, sir, is it true you will send all British soldiers home?"

General Carleton looked away. "I cannot say that for now."

"I hope it's true. We are tired of war, as you must be."

The general only nodded and rose from his desk. His aide handed James Mott the letter, which Anne's father placed in the leather pouch he carried on his shoulder.

"If you will excuse me, I must report to the prince," the general said, walking with them to the door and pointing far off. "That is he, astride the white horse near the largest tent."

Anne looked across the field in the direction the general pointed. She spotted the prince maneuvering his horse in some intricate patterns before an admiring audience. Without warning the horse reared up, almost unseating the prince. Anne could barely restrain her laughter. She was sure she would never forget the sight of that figure struggling to stay on his horse, that figure who might one day be king, but not her king!

Back home that evening, tired and weary from the long ride, she and Papa were surprised to find Captain Pete waiting for them.

"I was so caught up in getting the best of the British, I had no thought for a family that was good to me. Very reckless," he said, shaking his head. "Please forgive me." Anne knew those words did not come easily to the proud Captain Pete.

Papa was stern but gracious. "You went one step too far," he said, "and brought a vicious man to our home. You also used poor judgment in leaving Anne here alone. But I know you meant well and were a faithful worker for me in the past. So perhaps when the war is over, we can do business again."

After Captain Pete left, Papa and Anne sat down at the kitchen table. Jess had dug some clams and ground some corn, and Jinny had somehow made a meal from the two items.

"I was surprised to see Adam at Purchase," Papa told Anne. "He came to Meeting by way of Mamaroneck Harbor. In all the excitement I forgot to tell you. He comes for dinner tomorrow when he's finished with Meeting business."

"Oh," Anne said, barely able to suppress her excitement, "but he will be upset when he finds out what happened."

"I'm sure of that," Papa smiled.

I have nothing good to wear when he comes! Anne suddenly realized, remembering that the raiders had stolen her best dresses.

"Now we must go about recovering our possessions," Papa continued. "I'll send Jess early tomorrow with a few of the millhands. Let's hope he gets a favorable response."

It was late afternoon of the following day when Jess and the workers returned. Because Jess had been forced to stay with Merritt's men to help, he knew where most of the stolen goods had been distributed. The brigands had taken the booty to their homes some distance away or shared it with their friends.

Jess said that as soon as he showed the general's letter at each of the houses that morning, the ruffians grudgingly placed the Motts' possessions back in the cart. No one, not even Fade Merritt, dared disobey the direct order of so high a British general, especially one so close by. And Papa was sure when word got to him from General Carleton, he would leave the Motts alone in the future.

Anne drew a huge sigh of relief to see her finest gray linen dress in the pile of returned clothing that Jess had brought home. She smiled now as she began to understand the risk Rachel had taken. She no longer thought it was so frivolous to want a grand dress for your wedding, and she hoped the weather would be perfect for Rachel's big day.

Upstairs, she threw off her old homespun outfit and pulled her newly recovered best dress over her head, fastened it, and spun around, imagining that she was the one getting married. She slid the silver combs in her hair and patted it until it was perfect. Then placing the Quaker cap over her hair, she headed for the stairway.

Inspecting herself in the hall mirror, she saw Mama's face reflected back to her—the same deep blue eyes fringed with dark lashes, the same brown hair poking out from under her cap, and probably the silver combs underneath. *Just like me tonight!*

Downstairs, Anne grew restless as she waited in the parlor. *When did Adam leave Purchase?* she wondered. *When did he arrive at Mamaroneck Harbor? How long will it take him to sail down here?* It was almost dusk when she saw from the window a small white sail entering the cove.

"Adam's here! Adam's here!" Robert and Samuel called from outside. Any hope of seeing Adam alone for even a moment now was lost. Papa, hearing the news, came from his study and Richard from his room. Both were smiling and eager to talk over the latest Quaker matters with Adam, as well as the raid. Grandmother came from the kitchen, a smile in her eyes.

In minutes Adam strode into the room, his thick brown hair askew from the wind. Despite all the people around him clamoring for attention, his eyes were only for Anne.

"I just got word of the raid as I was leaving Purchase. I thought I would never get here! How are you, Anne?" he asked, his eyes full of concern.

"I'm fine now," Anne said quietly.

"Everybody was amazed at your courage. But I knew you were strong. I knew you could handle any situation. But I'm sorry you had to be alone," Adam said.

"Thank you," Anne replied, distracted. She wondered if anyone else could sense that Adam was speaking to her as more than just an old friend.

For the rest of the evening, Anne found her eyes

straying to Adam's face. During supper, she noticed that he was having as difficult a time concentrating on the conversation as she was.

It was not until it was time for Adam to leave that Anne finally had the chance to be alone with him. They walked slowly to the dock where his boat was tied. A brilliant silver half-moon made a ribbon of shimmering light on the cove waters. The air was cool and still and peaceful. The red mill was silent.

Anne removed her cap as they walked, and the moonlight glistened on the silver combs in her hair.

"I thank God you're safe," said Adam, gently touching the combs. "I see you are wearing these tonight. You must have been thinking the same thing as I—that your mother wore them the night she promised to marry your father." He paused and looked into her eyes. "I hoped you would be wearing them tonight, and I hoped it would mean that you would someday marry me."

"You did not hope in vain," she answered.

AUTHOR'S NOTE

Raid at Red Mill is the story of the Mott family who lived in the town of Mamaroneck in Westchester County during the American Revolution. It is based on a chapter in the book *Anne and Adam Mott, Their Ancestors and Descendants* by Thomas Cornell. Although this account has been fictionalized, with modifications and additions of minor characters and incidents, the basic facts of the story are true.

Not quite three years after the events in this novel, Anne, a few months shy of seventeen, married Adam Mott. Their marriage is recorded thus in the Purchase Monthly Meeting records:

> *19th of 5th mo., 1785*
> *At Mamaroneck meeting house, Adam Mott of Cowneck, township of North Hempstead, L.I., son of Adam,—to Anne Mott, of Mamaroneck, daughter of James.*

Anne raised five children and became an active member of the Quaker ministry. Her daughter-in-law was the famous abolitionist, Lucretia Mott. Fade Merritt was trapped and killed by whaleboatmen in New Rochelle in 1783.

SELECTED BIBLIOGRAPHY

- Bacon, Margaret Hope. *Valiant Friend: The Life of Lucretia Mott*. New York: Walker & Co., 1980.
- _____. *The Quiet Rebels—The Story of the Quakers in America*. Philadelphia: New Society Publishers, 1985.
- Brenner, Barbara. *If You Were There in 1776*. New York: Bradbury Press, 1994.
- Cooper, James Fenimore. *The Spy*. New Haven: College & University Press, 1971.
- Cornell, Thomas. *Adam and Anne Mott, Their Ancestors and their Descendants*. Poughkeepsie, NY: AV Haight, 1890.
- Dupuy, Trevor N. and R. Ernest. *The Compact History of the Revolutionary War*. New York: Hawthorn, 1963.
- Earle, Alice Morse. *Child Life in Colonial Days*. New York: Macmillan Co., 1961.
- Flexner, Helen. *A Quaker Childhood*. New Haven: Yale University Press, 1940.
- Hawke, David Freeman. *Everyday Life in Early America*. New York: Harper & Row, 1989.
- Hufeland, Otto. *Westchester County During the American Revolution*. New York: Harbor Hill Books, 1982.
- McGovern, Ann. *If You Lived in Colonial Times*. New York: Scholastic, 1992.
- Scharf, J. Thomas. *History of Westchester County*. Vol. 1. Philadelphia: L.E. Preston & Co., 1886.
- Sloane, Eric, ed., *Diary of an Early American Boy. Noah Blake, 1805*. New York: Ballantine, 1965.
- Wertenbaker, Thomas J. *Father Knickerbocker Rebels: New York City During the Revolution*. New York: Scribner's, 1948.